This book belongs to
the amazing, smart, and talented:

_____

To my former and current students— Wear your cape proud.
love yourself. and always be the best YOU that you can be!

Cultivating Positive Minds

Published by Cultivating Positive Minds, LLC.
Cincinnati, OH.

Paperback ISBN: 979-8-9856142-2-0
Hardcover ISBN: 979-8-9856142-0-6
Library of Congress Control Number: 2022905910

Cover and interior illustrations/design credit: Zach Orr

All inquiries of this book can be sent to the author.
For more information, please visit www.cultivatingpositiveminds.com

Self-Esteem: Feeling good about the type of person you choose to be.

Capes . . . They're for superheroes, right? Well, guess what? That's what we are!
We all have to be our own superhero before we can be anybody else's.

Everyone has an invisible cape they wear.
These capes that we wear help us become more CONFIDENT.

They give us the COURAGE to go through life feeling great about ourselves,
and they also help us reach our goals!

These capes help us realize that no matter what anybody else says, we are all different yet **AMAZING** individuals.

And with these capes, only **WE** can choose who we want to be and how we want to feel.

We can have as many capes as we feel we need, and the best part about these capes is that they come whenever we think positive thoughts or believe in ourselves.

There may be times in life when we look at other people and wonder why we don't have a cape like theirs . . .

. . . but then we remember that we can get a cape whenever we need it.
It just takes some believing in ourselves.

Sometimes, without even realizing it, people around us, such as our family, friends, teachers, and other people we're close with, will give us a piece of their cape that we may need.

. . . and that little piece may just go a long way.

There may be days when we don't feel like getting
our cape from someone else, and that's okay.

But when we get home and see all of our different capes laid out, we realize that we may have missed out—but we're going to wear one proudly the next day!

One day, you'll think you forgot your cape at home, and right before that test you're nervous about, you'll reach into your backpack and see it right there! You'll throw it on, right as your teacher is reminding you to write your name on your test.

And that test . . . well, that test is a piece of cake with the cape!

There will be times when we're nervous or scared to try new things.

But with our *BRAVE* cape on, we remember that everything we have done was once something new to us, but we were brave enough to try it anyway.

Sometimes, there will be people we come across that may try to bring us down about the things we wear, do, or create. They'll think their opinion matters.

But then we realize that we're wearing our CREATIVE cape and become proud of ourselves no matter what anybody else thinks.

There will also be times when we fail at something, but then we put our **TALENTED** cape on and remember we can do anything we put our minds to...

...and use that failure as an opportunity to get better.

Sometimes we may wonder why there's no one quite like us...

Then we remember we have our **UNIQUE** cape on. and we realize that being different from everyone else is the best part about ourselves!

Then one day, you'll realize you don't have to choose just one cape . . .
You can wear all of them at ONCE!

Even though our capes are invisible to everyone else,
trust me, others will know when we're wearing one!

These capes are magic, but they don't stop us from feeling bad all the time.
The most important thing is that we don't keep feeling bad for long.

SO, GO GET YOUR CAPE AND WEAR IT, PROUD AND STRONG!